MIDAS REX

IN CONNEMARA

James Kilcullen

ORIGINAL WRITING

ISBN:
Parent: 978-0-9571666-4-6
Epub: 978-0-9571666-5-3
Mobi: 978-0-9571666-6-0

A cip catalogue for this book is available from the National Library.

Published by Original Writing Ltd., Dublin, 2012.
Printed by Clondalkin Group, Glasnevin, Dublin 11

In a tense atmosphere in Teac Galway (assembly house) the leader of the opposition that well known cute hoor Moxy O'Shea, former Taoiseach, EU Commissioner, solicitor, TG for the kingdom of Kerry and all time gombeen man, rose to address the Teac. He knew he had Frank Carney, the Taoiseach (Prime Minister) on the ropes and could now force a General Election.

The visitors' gallery was packed and the press there in force; the TV cameras rolled. Ulick Joyc, first and only President of the Republic and still regarded as such by the people, sat quietly in the visitors' gallery. He was concerned for his old friend Taoiseach Frank Carney who was put in an indefensible position through no fault of his own.

For Moxy, the smartest politician in the house, it was pay back time; he had done a deal with three of the Government deputies; by the time this vote was taken farmer Carney could go back to milking cows. To mark the solemnity of the occasion he wore his new dark suit, white shirt and green tie; the Taoiseach sported the same old grey suit with a blue shirt and black tie.

Moxy looked around the chamber referred to his notes and began.

'Comairle (Speaker) I address this house at a time of great national crisis when, due to the negligence of the Taoiseach, our country is being deprived of billions of euro badly needed to improve our social services and renew our infrastructure. A foreign oil company has been given a license to develop the Sligo oil field and what do our people get: a miserable 1%.

Then he had the audacity to appoint a Minister for Energy, an outsider who is not a member of this house and not answerable to it. If I were the minister responsible I would solve this problem within seven days and require the exploiters of our natural resources to pay a royalty of at least 25% on every barrel of oil.

And where is the new railway line to Clifden and Roundstone that you promised at the last election? Taoiseach, I demand that you dissolve the Teac and put this matter to the people in a General Election.'

He sat down; great cheers came from his party members. Taoiseach Carney who had listened quietly to this blistering attack was finding it difficult to keep his temper; he rose slowly.

'Comairle, I'm pleased to hear that the members of the opposition are wearing their boots today. Moxy O'Shea well knows this concession was given by the Dublin Government before our State was set up. We all know the terms were ridiculous, but it was legal.'

He paused and looked around him.

'I am delighted to hear that Deputy O'Shea has the solution to our dilemma and could solve it within seven days. I'm so impressed that I propose to appoint Mr O'Shea to be our new Minister for Energy: he will be answerable to this house and I look forward to next week's meeting when I'm sure he will tell us how he solved this great national problem.'

He sat down amid cheers from his side of the house. Moxy tried to look confident as he was recognised by the Comairle.

'Comairle, it's not my function to hold the Taoiseach's hand; dissolve the house and hold a General Election.'

He sat down; the Taoiseach rose.

'Moxy do this for our people, you owe them that. Solve the problem in seven days and I'll gladly dissolve the house and go to the country.'

The government won the vote of confidence amid noisy exchanges; Moxy departed refusing to speak to the press.

***

Ulick Joyc, now a leading solicitor in the area, left his office and crossed the Main Street in Conna to Paulo's pub. He had arranged to meet Frank Carney and that old Connemara man, Ozzy. Tall and still handsome, well into his forties, Ulick lived in a modern bungalow out the Maam Cross road with his beautiful wife, Nodie and their two sons. A noted jurist, she was President of the Supreme Court.

Ulick and Frank were two of the founder members of the great Republic of Hi-Brasil when the western counties of Ireland broke away from Dublin to form a separate state within the EU. Its territory comprised the counties of Connacht; Galway, Mayo, Sligo, Roscommon and Leitrim; Counties Donegal, Clare, Limerick, Tipperary and Kerry. Cork refused to join when Galway was selected as capital.

Ozzy was there before him in the crowded bar where everyone was winding down after another day of immense inactivity. Dressed all in black with a shirt that was once white, he sported a bowler hat given to him many years ago by an English lord who owned an old mansion near Moycullen. It sat comfortably on his venerable head of white hair.

He was an affable old man with a small holding of land out the Lake Road; or so most people thought. Ulick knew differently; Ozzy was one of the Little Folk who lived in Rath Pallas near Lough Corrib. Not many people knew that. And they didn't know that his alter ego Dandaboy, (aka Danny) that little man all of thirty inches tall rarely manifested himself in public.

'What are you drinking, Mr President?' Ozzy asked smiling.

Ulick grunted. 'We'll have no arse licking here.'

Paulo stood before them. 'If there's to be any, I'll do it.'

'Let's have a couple of whiskies.'

Paulo Kelly was something of an institution in Conna. As a young man he left Carna, like many before him, took a job on one of the liners, eventually owned a saloon in Philadelphia before returning to Conna to fulfil his life's ambition; to own his own pub in his native Connemara. He bought Glynn's old place, refurbished the bar with the finest mahogany and lined the walls with pictures of the liners he worked on.

Drinks served, he stopped to talk.

'Did you ever see such fuckology in your life? The leaders of the EU running around in circles; it's one thing today and another tomorrow.'

'Don't lose any sleep over it, Paulo. Frank says it's all a game.'

With that Frank Carney entered the bar and was greeted with a loud cheer, which he acknowledged with a smile. A man of the people he insisted on being treated as an ordinary citizen, tolerated no nonsense and was well known for his caustic wit. Well on in years now, he lived with his partner in Westport; his wife died many years earlier and his two sons, both doctors, immigrated to Australia.

Ulick smiled. 'You're late Taoiseach.'

'I am that; I've just had a visit from Voncrap the CEO of Crap Oil.'

'Well then you need a large whiskey,' Paulo reached for the bottle.

'Are you making any progress with the bastard?'

'No. Despite the opposition of the locals he's got his damned oil rig up and running in Sligo Bay and boasted that he's now pumping 200,000 barrels a day.'

'Is there no way you can force him to give you a proper royalty?'

'No. He got a water tight contract from the bureaucrats in Dublin; defied me to try to break it.'

'So we're getting a miserable 1%; what are we getting from the Aran field.'

'35% and they're obeying all our safety regulations. Put them up again, Paulo.'

'Well, you saw Moxy off anyway.'

'It's that bastard Voncrap I'd like to see off.'

***

Ozzy headed out the lake road; it was a fine summer's evening with the noisy crows settling down for the night in the tall trees. Any day now the mayfly would be up and most of the people of Conna and Galway would head for the lake to fish for the world famous brown trout. Ozzy would not be joining them.

When he came to the Rath he blinked twice and there stood Danny, the impish faced little man dressed in a red tea shirt over green trousers; he walked through its grassy mound as if it didn't exist, waved to his friends going about their business and made his way down the wide street leading to the Imperial Square in front of the King's Palace.

He was the only one of his people permitted by Kingpa, King of the Little People, to stay in contact with the locals and help them whenever he could. He normally appeared in Public as Ozzy, but it was not unknown that he would appear as Danny. This unusual arrangement was devised hundreds of years ago when the local people were in dire straights and Kingpa decided to help them.

He entered the Palace and made his way to the throne room where the grand old man with flowing grey hair and a long white beard was waiting for him. He had taken off his crown to give his head a rest. Danny bowed and made his report; his master listened quietly. Not for the first time, Danny suspected that Kingpa was already aware of events.

'This Voncrap is surely a bad man.'

'He is majesty. Is there anything you can do to help our friends?'

He stroked his long beard.

'You will have to think about it.'

'Me?'

***

For Pat Ryan, manager at Shannon International Airport, the day started normally although his assistants noticed he appeared to be a bit apprehensive. It was a calm sunny day; he should be playing golf this morning. With aircraft coming and going all the time everything was normal until shortly before noon.

Then a giant Boeing 888 escorted by two fighter jets cruised in from the west and touched down on runway 23. The jets broke off. The plane came to a stop and taxied to the apron. A fleet of limos pulled up alongside and a Syrosky helicopter landed nearby.

Pat Ryan, standing in the tower, was approached by the customs chief.

'Is it true that these people have diplomatic immunity?'

'It is Mick.'

'I don't like being bypassed.'

'Neither do I.'

'Who is he?'

'I don't know; it's all very hush hush. We had a security team over here a month ago; they checked out the airport and the hotel in Connemara where our VIP will be staying. I've been on to the Taoiseach's office in Galway; they don't know anything or if they do they're not saying.'

'You didn't tell me.'

'It's top secret although I don't know why.'

While they watched, the steps were driven to the front exit and a number of suits, obviously security people, exited the plane first and got on board the helicopter which took off immediately. A tall mature looking man walked down the steps.

'Know him?'

'No, but he's not the US President or the Pope.'

***

Deep in the heart of Connemara the staff of Turla Lodge Hotel rushed around making sure that everything was in order. A magnificent old stone castle it was bought by the Order of the Fathers of the Brothers after the Great War. It was thought to be in communion with Rome, but it was unlikely Rome knew that. The good people of Connemara relaxed when it became clear these new Christians hadn't come to convert them. It was situated in the scenic heart of Maam valley with the Turk mountains to the rear and Lough Turla out front.

Lurglurg, the current Abbot was brought up on Inish Mor, one of the Aran Islands, and worked in England and on the roads of Connemara before joining the order. A big man with square features and completely bald, he was coming to grips with his nervous disposition; all he ever wanted to do was work on the farm, but despite his best efforts, failed in his attempt not to be elected abbot.

That was in the days when things were grim; they hardly had enough to eat. Then, Abbot Meskedra – sent by the Mother House or so he said – arrived and to Lurglurg's great joy, took charge. A man of many talents Meskedra converted the fine old castle into a luxury hotel.

He it was who introduced the regime of variable vows and took advantage of an old English Law that permitted the making of Poitin but forbid selling of it. A box at reception was marked "Offerings" and the size of the contribution was a good guide to the amount of Poitin you would receive. Room rates were adjusted to avoid embarrassing residents.

The hotel was a great success and, when Meskedra left with his fiancée, he insisted that Lurglurg be Abbot again.

***

When the hotel was visited by three suits who wanted to reserve it for a month, Lurglurg was very excited – at first. The fishing season wasn't going well. They produced pages and pages of their requirements in accommodation, food, drink and Internet links; even medical facilities although they would provide their own personnel. They talked and Lurglurg listened until they came to the bottom line: their unnamed client would deal with the hotel's account in six months time.

'Hold it right there,' He announced in high pitched tones. 'We will provide everything you need when the cash is in our bank.'

The youngish American – well, he spoke with an American accent – was outraged.

'We're talking here about one of the wealthiest men in the world.'

Lurglurg, the reluctant abbot, wasn't the brightest – and he knew it – but he'd heard that one before.

'If he's that well off then it won't be a problem.'

The head suit rose to depart; Lurglurg didn't move. The suit sat down again.

'All right. Make up your account. This is most irregular. My master will be displeased.'

***

Three days later a taxi pulled up outside Turla Lodge and a tall aristocratic looking gentleman dressed in black alighted, looked around him and walked into reception. Clean shaven with a carefully trimmed black moustache, luminous brown eyes and a well fitted black hair piece, he put on his glasses as he watched the taxi driver put down his bag beside him. Brother Brendan stood waiting patiently behind the desk, but his newly arrived guest was in no hurry.

'Welcome to Turla Lodge Hotel sir; have you a reservation sir?'

The man smiled. 'I am Senior Brother Angelo Pistroni from the Mother House here to see the Abbot Lurglurg.'

His accent was clearly Italian.

Brother Brendan got excited; the only one who ever knew anything about the Mother House was Abbot Meskedra and he was long gone.

'Welcome sir or should I call you Senior Brother?'

'Just call me Angelo, Brother Brendan.'

How the hell does he know my name?

'I'll take you to the Abbot right away – Angelo.'

Lurglurg was delighted to meet his new colleague; took him to his sitting room and ordered coffee. He wondered what he was doing here. In all his time in the order he had never heard anything from the Mother House; he often wondered if it still existed. Angelo sat back in the deep armchair and smiled.

'I've been sent by the Supreme Abbot to see how you are getting on since Abbot Meskedra departed.'

That was all right then.

'How is our revered Abbot Meskedra?'

'He's very well and sends his kindest regards to you and the brothers.'

'May I ask where he is?'

'In Jamaica; he set up a branch of the order there.'

This puzzled Lurglurg.

'Didn't he get married?'

'Oh yes. He has three children. Don't look so alarmed; our Jamaican house is old style Christian.'

'I hope you won't tell the brothers here; I have enough trouble running this place as it is.'

Angelo smiled. 'No, no. I'm here to watch and advise, not to cause you any trouble.'

Lurglurg wanted to ask how long he would be staying but didn't; that wouldn't be polite especially to a Senior Brother.

'Let me show you to the tower apartment; you'll be comfortable there.'

***

The limos, escorted by six outriders, arrived at Turla Lodge one hour after the helicopter touched down. They were followed by a coach carrying a mountain of luggage. Joseph L. Shulter, the VIP's general manager (gofor), a brisk, clean cut businessman who exuded authority, travelled with it. Lurglurg and his staff lined up to welcome and show them to their rooms. The security detail (all ex FBI) checked out the hotel, including a sweep for bugs, so they said, and then formed a guard of honour outside.

When the main party, which included a number of beautiful, expensively attired young ladies, arrived, Joe Shulter escorted the VIP to his suite on the third floor. When Brother Brendan was bold enough to ask him to sign the visitors' book he was ignored.

That did not impress the worthy brother; bad enough that he wouldn't sign in, and had the audacity to have this luxury hotel checked for bugs, the bloody bastard insisted on bringing his own chefs and domestic staff. And watching that line of beauties pass by was putting immense strain on his current variable vow of chastity. He could wind up having to go to confession!

The master, for that's what he was called, inspected his suite which was composed of large sitting and dining rooms, a master bedroom en suite looking out on the lakes and mountains of Connemara and an up to date office with phones, computers and Internet access.

He walked out on to the balcony and gazed at the beauty of his surroundings, but he saw only desolation. He knew his assistant had a pain to know why he came here, but he wasn't going to tell him. This was a man whose right hand didn't even know he had a left hand. He treated staff like mushrooms.

Herman Oberan was born in Boston – it was thought - of Dutch, German and Irish stock. The only child of doting parents he was destined for a bright and secure future. His correct title was Herman I. Oberan 111 but he had long since dropped the appendage as he insisted on being unique. People wondered what the "I" stood for; he wasn't about to reveal the obvious reference to a well known Middle Eastern race.

An introverted handsome young man – never popular with his mates - he studied Finance and Economics at Harvard, but took no part in sports. His great loves in life, then as now, were money, power and women. Much in demand he made the most of it.

Eventually, he married Elizabeth Maxwell, a beautiful young doctor from Chicago. They had two sons; Jack, a hippy artist in California who he rarely saw and Chester a playboy who did odd jobs for him but showed no real promise. Elizabeth divorced him when she discovered he was still playing the field. Now, at 59 he was faced with the problem of leaving it all to Chester. He couldn't let that happen.

The arrival of AIDS really scared him; he became a born again virgin over night, until he reorganised his life style. Now, he had five beautiful women with him at all times; his harem he called them; (high class hookers!) He paid them well for their lack of freedom; $20 million USD a year tax free. They could leave whenever they wished but not return.

As time passed he became obsessed with his health; so much so he employed a full medical team including two consultants who attended on him at all times. Although in the best of health he insisted on being examined every day; he could afford it so why not? He often asked himself the same question; am I satisfied with my life? The answer was no; there was one thing he needed and then he would be happy.

He entered his suite again.

'Shulter,' the master never used his Christian name – if he remembered it – 'What's the up to date position on the LIX shares?'

'They're down to $32 and falling.'

'Buy when they get to $30.'

'All 100 million.'

'Yes.'

After Shulter departed the master extracted a file from his briefcase, not one to which his chief of staff had access. It wasn't that he didn't trust his assistant; he didn't trust anyone.

LIX corporation was an up and coming oil exploration company which was about to hit the big time; it was also one of the few oil companies in which he didn't have a substantial stake. That was contrary to the Monopoly laws now in operation in many countries.

Operating world wide through hundreds of companies and intricate cross shareholdings, he regarded monopoly laws with great respect otherwise he would have had them abolished. They were for the amateurs and prevented them from ever getting into the big league.

A master file of all his holdings and properties around the world was locked away in a secure safe; he wouldn't permit the details to be put on computer. He kept a summary in a little black book that he carried with him at all times. It was such a colossal financial web that he had to consult it regularly. A copy was held by his lawyers in New York.

His empire was a pyramid that spread out from a private holding company at its peak, registered in Cayman and descended into an intricate web of Corporations. And not one share or property was held in his own name. He owned the world; well most of it, but the world didn't know that.

He built up an international network of highly paid agents who monitored the major stock markets; Tokyo, Hong Kong, London and Wall Street. They scrutinised all interesting transactions and filed weekly reports. This information often included activities in the master's companies, but they only knew what they were told. Part of their remit was to watch the ups and downs in the markets; to sell at the top and buy at the bottom. It went on all the time and yielded a profit of about a Billion a month.

Two weeks earlier he instructed one of his Chinese companies to sell 100 million LIX shares; at that time they were quoted at

$67 USD. This was followed by a prepared Wall Street rumour that LIX was having trouble with its accounts and there was some suggestion that certain assets were being kept off the balance sheet.

As he well knew, nothing travels faster than rumour. His old father often postulated; "What was the first thing man did when he came out of the cave? No, not that, he panicked." The share price dropped as anticipated. Once the price hit $30 USD he would buy in to complete the contract. It was standard short selling; he sold 100 million shares he didn't own at $67 USD a share and would buy 100 million at $30 USD; making a net gain of about $4 Billion.

What to do with his profit? Invest it in LIX shares. A succession of such transactions would eventually give him a substantial holding in a valuable company for one or two million dollars in fees. It's simply using suckers money, but that's what suckers are for.

Three governments had the audacity to make short selling illegal; they even tried to regulate derivates. He soon put a stop to that. Who do those petty politicians think they are?

***

Joe Shulter, a native of California, majored in Law at Berkeley before setting out on a distinguished career in the SEC, Wall Street and as Personal Assistant to the late President. It was during his time in the White House that he met his current master, a man so wealthy that the President almost genuflected in his presence. And yet he was little known outside a select number of financial people; it was thought he was an American of European extraction but he neither confirmed nor denied it.

The master firmly believed it was essential that he maintained a low profile; the less people knew about him the better; his photo never appeared in any newspaper or magazine; he gave no interviews; his many mansions around the world were secluded and well guarded. He didn't make enemies: his companies did. His great fear was assassination.

Shulter knew his master didn't trust him, but as he was being paid $500 million USD tax free a year he could live with that. When he had enough he would retire and return to California with the woman he loved; discretion was necessary for the present; he had just divorced his third wife.

While setting up his own office he took a call from the US ambassador in Galway; could he call to pay his respects to the master? Not yet. Was the master here to deal with the euro crisis? Couldn't comment sir. He hung up the phone. It was always his practice to infer knowledge when he had no idea what was happening; an old White House practice.

**

Edwardo Capitalo, the dapper new chairman of the ECB, (European Central bank) a Czech career economist, was quite nervous when he arrived at Turla to see the master. As the situation was rapidly becoming critical again, he flew into Knock at short notice. If the euro wasn't rescued quickly he would be looking for another job. The master received him in his office.

Shulter left them alone or so he thought; Danny was wandering around looking up at Midas who listened in silence to his visitor's plea.

'Mr Oberan, sir, we need your help if the euro is to survive.'

He appeared to consider it.

'The downfall of the euro would be a great disaster. You may issue bonds to the value of four Trillion euro at 4% interest for the first five years increasing to 7% on the balance then due.'

'Oh thank you sir.'

'Don't thank me yet; there is one condition.'

'Yes sir.'

'Friends of mine are anxious to take a stake (his word for control) in NuclearE, (the world's largest and most advanced manufacturer of nuclear fusion plants) which is based in Hamburg. Their offer has been rejected; I think the board should reconsider because I can't proceed with the bonds until it's accepted.'

Capitalo frowned. 'I know the German Chancellor is totally opposed to this takeover and his Government owns 60% of the company.' He paused. 'Would you consider increasing the offer, sir?'

He shook his head. 'My friends are adamant; NuclearE accepts this offer or the euro is finished. And if the euro goes how long will NuclearE last?'

'May I ask sir, should the euro fail what would it be replaced by? The US Dollar?'

'No, the Chinese Yuan.'

He was flabbergasted. 'We can't have that, sir.'

The master became impatient.

'You've got to have something and fast; this crisis has gone on for far too long. Resolve it today or I'll talk to the Chinese.'

An interesting comment from the man who stoked up the crisis and had, so far, made Billions out of it.

'Can I ring Herr Lutzgart?'

The master stood up. 'The phone is there. Tell my assistant when you've consulted your people.'

He left the room.

Danny, who had no idea of what was going on, listened while the distraught Capitalo held a lively conversation with the German Chancellor. He finally summed up. 'We have to keep the Chinese out.'

The tone of the conversation improved and with perspiration pouring off his forehead Capitalo hung up.'

***

He stayed for lunch. The master was at his most pleasant, as well he should be, and by the time coffee was served Shulter handed him a printed copy of an email received from his New York lawyers. The deal was done. The master rose and shook hands with the relieved Capitalo.

'It's a pleasure to do business with you, Edwardo, isn't it? May I suggest that the NuclearE takeover remain secret?'

'I'm sure the Chancellor would like that, sir.' He paused. 'When can we announce the issue of the Bonds?'

'As soon as you return to Frankfort this evening send the details to my lawyers in New York; it will only be mid afternoon there. You should be ready to go public first thing tomorrow morning before London and New York open.'

'Would it be a good idea to put a further Trillion in reserve?'

The master smiled. 'I'll arrange that, on the same terms of course. What will you do with Greece now?'

'We plan to give them another €200 Billion with strict instructions to get their act together.'

'Why not let them default or better still kick them out of the common currency?'

'If we put them out now they would be followed by at least three other countries. That would be the end of the euro.'

'So what do you plan?'

'We've got to get all other member countries back on track. Then we'll get rid of Greece; there's no way they will ever sort themselves out. They can go back to the Drachma.'

The master nodded. 'Seems like a good plan. You do realise that the ECB will be responsible to my Bond holders for all sums advanced plus interest, regardless of how you deal with your member states.'

'Of course sir.'

The master smiled.

'I have every confidence in you Edwardo. I'll have one of my drivers take you to the airport.'

***

He returned to his office; there would be Billions to be made – when Greece departed - as he discovered when Russia and Argentina defaulted. Financial control of Iceland was on his agenda, but first things first.

He emailed the following message to a number of his stock exchange agents: "Immediate. Buy European stocks as per you're A list. Spend up to $100 Billion and keep me advised."

Then he sent the following message to his derivates companies: "Immediate. Back the euro."

Capitalo's announcement would be followed by a spending spree such as not seen before on world stock markets. He would make at least a Trillion over the next two weeks.

Greece would certainly default probably followed by two or three other EU countries. He emailed his Insurance Broker in New York; cover default of any or all EU countries. When Greece defaulted the ECB would cover his losses and so would his insurers.

The NuclearE purchase was sweet; no way would the Germans let it go until they had to. He had already bought a hundred European companies at knock down prices. The Athens subsidiary of his Boston bank would now be recapitalised and become solvent again; time to sell it on while the going was good. When Greece defaulted he would buy it back for a pittance, recapitalise it and control the country's finances for the future.

In his own office, Shulter was getting in on the act; he bought a considerable number of shares for his own account and then tipped off his friends in New York and Washington.

The master took a number of calls from wealthy associates; everyone in the upper echelons of finance knew that Capitalo had a secret meeting with him in Connemara. But they didn't know the outcome and the master advised caution; it was still in the balance; best wait for Capitalo's announcement. As always he held the pole position; he had covered all the squares.

Now, he could devote some time to the purpose of his visit to Connemara.

Danny's head was spinning when he departed.

***

Hundreds of protesters assembled in the village of Grange where the Voncrap refinery was currently pumping thousands of tons of crude oil into waiting tankers. The crowds were getting smaller; after years of protest the battle was lost; they knew that. Their tourist trade was destroyed. Two sympathetic local guards stood by; there wouldn't be any trouble. A helicopter carrying Voncrap flew over the protesters on course to the oil rig ten miles off shore.

***

The Taoiseach's arrival at Turla was greeted with great respect by Lurglurg and the brothers; Shulter was polite but business like and showed him into the master's presence after a fifteen minute wait. Frank was amused as he surveyed the security people who were obviously armed. A sign outside read "No Visitors." Danny, unseen, was disgusted at the lack of respect shown to his Taoiseach.

Shown into the master's office, Shulter introduced him and left wondering what his master was doing with such low life. The master waved Frank to a chair without offering to shake hands with him.

'You have in this area a race of people with extraordinary powers,' he didn't waste time on preliminaries.

'We have many exceptional people,' he replied.

Another stupid politician the master thought.

'I'm referring to the Little People who live near the town of Conna.'

'That's true.'

Doesn't he have any idea of who I am; he doesn't even call me "sir?" Time to come to the point.

'I'm probably the wealthiest man on this planet. I have everything except the one thing which your friends can give me.'

Frank stayed silent; the master produced a folded sheet of paper and handed it to him.

'This is what I require; I want you to see your friends and arrange it for me.'

Frank opened the sheet and read the contents; Dan edged closer to have a gawk; he nearly collapsed. The Taoiseach folded the paper and handed it back.

'Your visit here is unnecessary; the Little People won't agree to this.'

The master was unfazed. 'They will do it for me.'

Frank merely shook his head.

The master was getting angry now.

'I'll tell you why they will do it; because if they refuse me I'll have this country bombed out of existence.'

Frank rose, wondering if he had accidently strayed into a lunatic asylum.

'My people don't like threats; I'll bid you good day.'

As he left the room the master screamed after him. 'I don't make threats.'

It suddenly occurred to him; once he got what he required, and he was sure he would, he couldn't permit anyone else to have it.

***

Lurglurg, accompanied by Angelo Pistroni met the Taoiseach in reception. The unseen Danny looked closely at the Senior Brother while Lurglurg introduced him. The little man was puzzled; where have I seen this fellow before?

Angelo was at his most affable. 'Taoiseach, will you join me for a drink?'

'Certainly.'

Lurglurg showed them to a comfortable lounge and left them. Brother Brendan served large brandies. While Angelo knocked it back like a veteran, Frank sipped it slowly; glad he had brought his official driver. Angelo, to Brother Brendan's astonishment called for another and dispatched it with a noble flourish. To be fair to Frank he did his best to keep up, but soon realised he was on a loser; he should have opted for Poitin.

Danny left them. Angelo lowered his voice so that Brother Brendan couldn't hear him.

'Taoiseach, I'm here on a special mission.'

'So Lurglurg tells me.'

'Not that one. Can I call to your office tomorrow? I'd like to have a chat with you.'

'By all means.'

He was wondering if the bould Angelo would be sober by tomorrow; more immediately, would he be able to walk out of here without dishonouring his office? They were still at it when Danny returned; Frank had fallen far behind but Angelo was in full swing. The little man could only conclude that the ability to knock back brandy like that must have been part of Angelo's religious training.

When Frank finally stood up to commence the long walk to his car he didn't realise he was being supported by the unseen Ozzy.

***

The Russian ambassador presented his card, bowed before the master and took a seat in the sitting room.

'You sent for me, sir?'

'Yes,' he looked at the card, 'Oleg. I would like you to convey my good wishes to your President and tell him I'm concerned about the extent of military activity in Mongolia, near your Siberian border with China. My sources tell me that secret plans to invade your country have been drawn up in Beijing. They want your oil fields.'

'That is alarming sir. Are you sure?'

'Regrettably, yes. They need the oil. They've started stockpiling weapons including missiles; have even built three aircraft carriers.'

The ambassador rose. 'I'll travel to Moscow and report directly to our President.'

'Tell him that in the event of conflict my armaments factories will refuse to supply China.'

He bowed. 'I'm most grateful, sir.'

***

Ozzy, after two pints and a whiskey, was in good form when he left Paulo's and headed out the road home. He didn't notice the big black limo until it pulled up beside him; two men jumped out, grabbed him and pushed him into the rear seat. He was pinned between two heavies; it took him a while to work out what was happening as the car headed out into Connemara.

He decided to go along with it; arriving at the hotel he was locked in a basement room. Making himself invisible he made his way to the master's suite where he was entertaining one of his ladies. It was time to have some fun. He let one of the guards see him and promptly disappeared.

There was consternation with suits shouting and running around looking for him; he was really enjoying this; now you see him, now you don't. Eventually, they checked his cell; he was sitting there quietly. When they left he started wandering again; they couldn't figure it out. Every time they checked his cell he was there.

When they came for him in the morning he wasn't there; he was but they couldn't see him. Consternation again! He wandered around causing further panic. Then he walked through reception and out into the car park. Visible now, he watched while six guards approached; he backed away slowly until he was standing at the edge of the lake.

'We have the bastard now,' Hank, the head honcho swore.

Ozzy smiled, turned and walked out on the lake; Brother Brendan came out to see what all the commotion was about. Digital cameras were clicking all around him.

'Jaysus, he can walk on water.'

Fifty yards from dry land Ozzy turned and smiled at them. His guards just stood there wide eyed. The master watched from his balcony; Angelo from the tower.

'He's walking on water,' Hank couldn't believe his eyes.

'It's been done before,' Brother Brendan enthused, 'But not for sometime.'

Ozzy walked on; two hundred yards out, he turned, doffed his bowler, bowed and disappeared.

The master was impressed.

'Those pictures will be worth a fortune,' Hank fiddled with his digital camera.

'Shit,' one of his men swore, 'He doesn't appear in any of them.'

The only camera showing Ozzy walking on water was Angelo's.

***

The US ambassador couldn't believe his ears.

'Let me get this right sir; you want the US to bomb this country?'

'That's exactly right. Fly to Washington and convey my order directly to President Polatley. A missile or air raid attack wiping out Galway might do.'

The worried looking diplomat rose.

'I'll report to the President right away sir.'

'You do that. Would you like a brandy before you leave?'

'No thank you sir.'

***

The Chinese ambassador, Han Wong was very nervous when shown into the presence of the master; he was only a tiny cog in a very big wheel and wasn't used to being so honoured.

The master didn't waste time.

'I'm very concerned about some news picked up secretly by my agents in Moscow. Russia is planning to attack your country through Mongolia, which it claims to own. My sources tell me they're stockpiling missiles and currently carrying out military exercises. I suggest you travel to Beijing immediately and acquaint your chairman.'

Han Wong rose. 'I'll travel today sir.'

'And be sure to tell him that in the event of hostilities, I will not support Russia.'

'Thank you sir,' he bowed and departed.

Left on his own the master smiled as he sipped his brandy. Prospects of conflict – so easily encouraged - were always good for business and would keep his armament factories in full production. With weaponry being upgraded all the time there were always buyers in the market.

He had no direct interest in manufacturing, but armaments were different; they yielded the highest profit margins of any commodity on earth with no advertising costs or difficulty getting cash in advance. Some of the world's tin pot dictators were among his best customers.

Now what should he do about the Middle East? The unseen Danny put his hand on the master's wrist and learned the contents of the great man's mind. He departed in a state of shock.

***

When Ozzy met Ulick and Frank in Paulo's he brought them up to date and ended: 'I know not what happening except this man is mad; he told the Americans to wipe us out.'

'Does he seriously think America would do that?' Ulick asked.

27

'He does, but I don't think America would be that foolish,' Frank replied.

'What a thought! He wants to become ruler of the world.' He turned to Ozzy. 'What does Kingpa think?'

'Kingpa says this man is already ruler of the world.'

Frank summed up. 'There is no way this loony can be given what he wants.'

Paulo stood before them.

'I see the euro problem has been solved again.'

'Paulo,' Frank replied. 'I always told you it was a game. Once the big money – the bondholders - could make no more out of frightening the daylights out of the people, they were bound to come up with the money. They never wanted to bring down the euro; it wouldn't pay them.'

Ozzy put down his glass. 'What bondholders?'

Frank smiled. 'It's a lovely name to conceal Big Money; including drug barons, dictators, gangsters, money launderers, subversive organisations, you name it; they're all there hidden under that fancy and harmless title. The ECB (European Central Bank) issued bonds for four Trillion euro to organisations controlled by our friend out in Turla. They don't want to know where the money is coming from.'

'What Trillion?' Ozzy asked.

'Written down it's 1 followed by noughts running down to the end of the bar,' Ulick, who had no idea, replied.

That didn't satisfy Ozzy. 'What you think Frank?'

He produced his diary and started scribbling.

'A million is a thousand thousand (1,000,000); a Billion is a thousand million (1,000,000,000) and a Trillion is a thousand Billion (1,000,000,000,000) I think.'

'You see,' Ulick insisted, 'I was right.'

Ozzy tried to get his head around these figures.

'So, the money people send euro to the big bank in Frankfurt; wouldn't it need ships with millions of sacks full of notes?'

Frank intervened. 'No Ozzy, it doesn't work like that. The bank in Frankfurt just puts the figure of four Trillion in their computer as a credit and everyone is happy.'

'But they haven't got the money?' Ozzy was getting even more confused.

'They don't need the money because they won't be using it.'

'You've lost me too,' Ulick added while Paulo put up three more drinks.

'Some years ago most of the banks in the world followed the American lead and went mad giving out loans; they did this by showing debits in their own accounts and credits in the borrowers' accounts. Very little actual cash changed hands.

They knew the day of reckoning would come, but they didn't care; governments would bail them out because they were too big to be allowed fail. One senior banker in the US said: "We have to keep dancing until the music stops." He didn't realise the music had long since stopped. As always, the bill was passed to the hoi polloi, the great unwashed, little people like us.'

***

Voncrap's helicopter circled the oil rig and sat down gently on the helipad; the great man was furious. The tall mature Texan had bluffed and bullied his way to the top of the oil business. He founded, sold shares to the public and became CEO of his own company – now a substantial corporation - to develop the Sligo oil field.

As he alighted he was approached by the rig manager Ernie Williams, a mild mannered elderly man with considerable experience in the oil business.

'What the hell do you mean sending for me at this hour of the morning? What's wrong?' he demanded.

Williams replied. 'I've never seen anything like this before sir; everything was normal until three o'clock; then we started pumping water.'

'What the hell do you mean? Water?'

'We've checked the seismograph. All indications are that the well has bottomed out.'

'That's not possible; there's a hundred Billion barrels down there. It can't just disappear.'

'I agree sir. Our engineers are working on it. This is our first experience of drilling in the Atlantic shelf.'

'You'd better come up with something fast; if this gets out our shares will go through the floor. No one leaves the rig and not a word to the press.'

***

The master let Shulter finish.

'Let me get this right: a Hong Kong Industrialist, Kin Lee, sold 50 million shares in one of our companies and has put out a rumour about an SEC investigation. By how much have the shares fallen?'

'$100 USD so far.'

Kin Lee could not be expected to know that one of the master's corporations controlled this asset.

'Put a buy order on those shares; take up any that become available at any price. Get me a full report on this fellow's activities. I'll fix the bastard.'

'Yes sir.'

'Tell the SEC to deny any such rumours and the rating agencies to confirm our AAA rating.'

'Yes sir.'

***

Danny found a very relaxed Senior Brother Angelo Pistroni sitting at his laptop composing an email; he stood beside him and watched for a while. The email sent; the little man let the worthy brother see him. He grinned and put out his hand.

'Dan – the - boy, I was wondering when you would show up; it's great to see you again.' He paused and grinned mischievously. 'I hope you won't unmask Angelo.'

Danny smiled; he liked this man who he once distrusted.

'You honest man; is Angelo honest man?'

'No, he's the world's greatest conman.'

Honest men always tell the truth; Danny surely knew this was the truth.

'Danny needs advice.'

'You've come to the right man.'

***

Shulter returned later.

'Russia has secretly moved troops to the Chinese border. They're looking for the latest technology; missiles, Leopard tanks, Bronco armoured troop carriers and F-16 fighters for a start. Our factories need your permission to supply.'

'Give Singapore and Birmingham the go ahead. They should refuse any orders from China.'

'Does that mean you won't supply China, sir?'

'No, we'll supply China directly from the South Korean plant in Puson.'

'Very astute sir, if I may say so.'

'You may. Now, tonight I want Anne; will you tell her to report in at nine?'

'Yes, sir.'

***

The US ambassador was very nervous; he knew the master wouldn't like the message he came to Turla to deliver. Privately, he wondered what the master required from a small backward country like Hi-Brasil. He was put sitting down and offered a coffee which he was pleased to accept; anything to put off the dreaded moment.

'Well.' The master inquired when the coffee was served. 'When will the President take the action I want?'

'I'm afraid sir, the President is very disturbed by your suggestion; we have nothing against this country - at the moment - that would justify such a step.'

He finished his coffee; he wouldn't be offered another one.

The master didn't raise his voice.

'Go back to President Polatley and ask him who put him in the White House three years ago and would he like to be re-elected next year?'

***

Shulter went to the wing of the hotel where the ladies were kept separately, under the supervision of two guards. Why two? The master wouldn't trust one. After all they were beautiful ladies. Twice a week they were taken by coach on shopping trips which they enjoyed; outside their quarters they were escorted by four guards. They descended on the Galway shops like locusts, bought rings round them and even flirted with the shop assistants.

Shulter was checked into the wing by one of the guards who duly noted it in his manual; he knocked politely on Anne's door and was admitted. Once he closed the door behind him, she threw herself into his arms and they kissed longingly; she was wearing a very revealing pink negligee.

'Take me, love,' she panted and boy was he up for it.

'It's too dangerous, my love.' He whispered.

'I lie awake at night longing for you. When are we going to get out of this prison?'

'It won't be long now.'

'Haven't we enough money.'

He smiled. 'We have; the euro shares have gone through the roof.'

He became nervous.

'I've got to go. I've been here too long. Be patient, my love. He wants you at nine.'

They kissed again and he departed.

***

Following Shulter's representations the master finally agreed to grant an interview to Senior Brother Pistroni; he wouldn't have if he knew what it was about. Angelo was at his most affable and ignored the fact that he wasn't asked to sit down or offered a coffee.

'What is it you want?' he asked briskly. People always wanted something from him.

'Sir,' Angelo was a past master of the art, 'Our order runs a charity called Africa Aid. As you know the droughts in the continent are getting worse and causing considerable loss of life and great hardship.'

The master frowned; another fucking charity.

Angelo continued. 'Last year sir you were kind enough to donate one million dollars. I know times are hard, but would you find it in your generous heart sir to increase your subscription to say ten million this year?'

'Why don't those people get off their arses and make use of their own resources? Oh all right, I'll increase it to five million. I'll have Shulter deliver the cheque to you.'

'Thank you kindly sir.'

Angelo's thoughts as he departed could not be expressed in polite society.

The visit reminded the master of his need to take action regarding some of his assets. Clearly climate change was becoming more serious in areas between the tropics. He should unload his major interests there while prices were still good. The Chinese would help here; they were particularly interested in Africa. He consulted his little black book.

He had acquired and recapitalised a small local bank in Iceland where there was an ongoing debate about the country's future currency. The Krona was no longer in favour; the country was equally divided between the Canadian Dollar (known as the Loonie) and the euro. This country would become more important as global warming forced more people to move north. He decided the country would best be served by the US Dollar.

Which reminded him; had his London lawyers finalised the purchase of 500,000 acres of land near Malmo in northern Sweden?

**

The story broke in New York the following morning; it was world news. VONCRAP IRISH WELL BOTTOMS OUT AFTER 2 MILLION BARRELS. Denials from the Head Office and Sligo were so contradictory they went unheeded; the shares tanked.

In Sligo the engineers confirmed to Voncrap that the well had indeed dried up. He screamed at them. 'Oil doesn't just disappear; find it or I'll sack the lot of you.'

**

The master's son, Chester arrived the following day from New York. Tall and handsome like his father, yet all he ever learned was how to spend money. He had never been close to his father, a remote, cold and distant figure. In his six years in Columbia University he had a great time gambling and entertaining the ladies. He had inherited something from his father after all. His mother remarried and was now living in Miami.

Chester had a problem and was apprehensive of his father's reaction to it; his gambling debts were way over the top and his bookies left him in no doubt; get the money or else. His income from his father was only three million a month, not nearly enough for a man with several lady friends and bookies to support.

The master saw him alone in his lounge and listened to his tale of woe.

'You want me to pay those shysters a Billion dollars? Are you mad?'

'If you don't; I'm dead.'

'You go back to those bums and tell them that if they lay a hand on you I'll turn the FBI on them.'

'Will you double my allowance?'

'No.'

He stood up. 'Goodbye father.'

He left for the airport in Galway.

***

Frank had an official visit from the elderly US ambassador Robb Delray, a one time New York stock broker and friend of President Polatley. This surprised him; these gentlemen spent most of their time partying, bed hopping or playing golf. It's unlikely old Delray went in for bed hopping, but then you never can tell!

'Taoiseach,' he began hesitantly. 'The President would like you to comply with Mr Oberan's request.'

Clearly he didn't know what it was.

'No way,' he replied not being given to diplomatic niceties.

'The President is most earnest, sir.'

'That fellow out in Turla; is he god?'

He took a deep breath.

'I'm afraid he is sir.'

'And what happens if we don't comply?'

'I don't know sir.'

***

Now that the master controlled NuclearE – through a little known company in Rio - he instructed it to resume supplies to Iran; a facility cut off after the German Government reacted to demands from Israel. He had decided that Iran should have nuclear power – at a price - and if that included the bomb, so be it. It was time for Israel to get real; give the Palestinians their pre 67 territory and put an end to the continued conflict in the area.

He had just learned that Israel was seeking a large supply of armaments from his US factories via Washington; he authorised it with a long delivery date; the US would pay for it. Israel was planning to attack Iran. If that was permitted Iran would close the gulf of Hermuz and a world oil shortage would follow. That might not be a bad result; the price of oil would rocket; his oil companies would do well out of it.

On the other hand if Russia and China became involved, as they might, it could result in a world war. Such conflict would upset financial stability; it becomes more difficult to control the situation once the shooting starts. Russia and China were sufficiently occupied at the moment eyeing up one another across their common border.

He gave instructions to the US President that under no circumstances should Israel be allowed attack Iran. At the same time he ordered his Chinese factory to supply Iran with whatever armaments they required. This would be an opportunity to get rid of some of the older stock currently held in Shanghai.

***

As the Boeing 777 flew across Canada en route to Las Vegas, Chester became angrier with his father; the bloody bastard was one of the wealthiest men in the world; a Billion dollars was chicken feed to him. He would have it all one day; all he had to do was outlive the old bastard.

That process could be speeded up. His fertile mind began to consider how that might be achieved. It wouldn't cost that much and it would keep his creditors off his back in the meantime; a dead man would be of no use to them.

***

When Frank arrived in Paulo's he shook Ozzy by the hand.

'We found out what you did with the oil; it's now 75 miles further north off the Donegal coast. How did you do it?'

'Ozzy not know; ask Danny.'

Ulick intervened smiling. 'Just because you walk on water doesn't entitle you to act the bollocks with our Taoiseach.'

Frank grinned. 'It's all right; I'll forgive him this time.'

Ozzy tried to look chastened.

***

Shulter reported in, holding a file which he handed to the master.

'Kin Lee owns 40% of the biggest bank in Hong Kong, sir.'

'What are our shares at now?'

'We've bought everything available; we're now five points above the price he sold them for and settlement day is tomorrow.'

'So, it will cost the bastard Billions to fulfil his contract. But that's not the end of it.'

'What have you got in mind sir?'

'Deposit $100 Billion HKD in his bank on a withdrawal on demand basis.'

Not knowing what the master was up to now he merely said: 'Yes sir,' and departed.

***

The master took a phone call from US Secretary of State Martha Kevioni on a secure line; he listened carefully before replying.

'No, Madam,' he was always respectful. 'You can't let Israel attack Iran. I'm not concerned about casualties; world oil supplies would be affected and I don't think China and Russia would stand by.'

'You think they would attack Israel?'

'I wouldn't rule it out; Iran is China's principal supplier of oil.'

'And if Israel refuses?'

'Tell them they're on their own; it's time they talked to their enemies instead of hiding behind their friends.'

'Would a separate state of Palestine appease Iran?'

'Madame Secretary, instruct Israel to get rid of that stupid wall and give the entire West Bank back to Palestine.'

'Are you aware that NuclearE in Hamburg has resumed supplying Iran with nuclear facilities?'

'No.'

'What do you think would happen if Israel goes ahead and attacks Iran?'

'Iran would wipe Israel off the face of the map but not before Israel used the bomb.'

'You think it would be that bad?'

'I do.'

He changed the subject.

'When are you planning to attack Galway?'

'I'm using diplomacy whilst looking for some excuse to launch hostilities.'

'Don't take too long.'

***

With energy, banking and government financing wrapped up, the master turned his attention to water; it was rapidly becoming scarcer and more expensive. He studied reports of the five large desalination plants in operation around the world; two of them in the US. This would be a good time to invest and at the same time provide them with whatever loan capital they required. Within five years he would control this business. He sent an email to his New York stock broker.

Government leaders always insisted their countries must live within their means and then went off and borrowed more. The idea of repaying any of the National Debts was anathema; it was best not to talk about them; the people wouldn't understand anyway.

The master and his friends didn't want any country to repay their debts; where else could they lend such sums with security and a guaranteed return? And when loans were repaid they were immediately replaced by new ones.

He smiled when he watched the all important world leaders on TV, strutting across the stage of history, making big speeches impressing the people with their dedication to economic prosperity and world peace, followed by photo calls, TV interviews, surrounded by lackeys and travelling in executive jets. They were full of wind; and all the time they were merely puppets carrying out their masters' instructions. It had its advantages; it enabled him to stay in the background.

Impressions are important. In a recent high profile case in New York a leading dealer was convicted of insider trading and sent to jail for fifteen years. That was good for the morale of business; the people would now have more confidence in the system, little realising it was window dressing; everyone in financial circles was involved in insider trading. There was nothing wrong with it.

***

Ozzy was becoming more and more puzzled and he wasn't the only one. When they met again he expressed his confusion to Ulick and Frank.

'How did this bubble, as you call it, work?' He asked.

Frank put down his glass.

'It was a bubble that grew into a colossal balloon; US institutions mostly owned by Big Money lent money to people who had no possibility of repaying it, and they knew that. The more loans they made the more money they made; it became a Trillion dollar industry. They sold the loans to investment banks; this was called securitizion (a system meant to provide security) and there ended the lenders involvement.

The investment banks packaged hundreds of sub prime loans with car loans, personal loans etc - at a time – now called derivatives, and sold them to investors all around the world. The borrowers were now required to repay their loans to the investors; the balloon just kept growing.

Borrowers defaulted in their thousands; investors lost Billions. What was happening was so obvious that the FBI issued a warning. Property prices doubled. I think it was all a money making racket from the start.'

'It was more sophisticated than anything we've seen before,' Ulick took up the story. 'The investment banks took out insurance against borrowers defaulting, covering themselves against failure which they knew would come. They became worried that their insurance company – the biggest in the world – would be unable to meet their losses and took out insurance against that company going bust.

The insurance company did go bust; was taken into public ownership; cost the taxpayers nearly $180 Billion USD. The investment banks were paid in full and the now virtually state owned Insurance Company was required to waive its rights to sue the banks. It doesn't get any better than that.'

'Were there no laws to prevent such skulduggery?'

'Efforts to introduce control of this 50 Trillion USD derivative Juggernaut were quickly withdrawn under pressure from the banks and Wall Street. They were making Billions out of it. Let's face it; Washington – like many other capitals – is run by Big Money. They call the shots; legislators bow the knee.'

'What derivatives?' Ozzy asked.

'You may well ask,' Frank replied. 'You can take out a derivative on anything; shares rising or falling, the weather; the races; it's a dangerous form of unregulated gambling; you can back the horse to win and then back him to lose, if you have the money. Fifty people could take out a derivative on my house – in which they have no interest – and if it burns they get paid.'

'That's crazy.'

'It is, but Big Money still makes Trillions out of it.'

'Were there no regulators?'

'Oh yes, the SEC (Securities and Exchange Commission) but they didn't want to know and later claimed they were short of staff. And they ignored several written warnings about Bernie Madoff's Ponzi scheme; received ten years before he put up his hands.'

'What about the rating agencies?'

Ulick smiled. 'They gave AAA (the highest) and AA ratings to organisations up to a few days before they went bust. Remember Enron! When the balloon went up they were required to appear before Congressional committees at which they said their ratings were only opinions and not to be relied upon. They made Billions too; the higher their ratings the more they received.'

'Why have rating agencies?'

'Why indeed.'

'So they were all in it together.'

'And they made Billions which they weren't required to repay.'

'And no one was even arrested never mind put in jail.' Ulick paused. 'The worrying part is they are still there. A leading

American described the whole episode as a great big national and not just national, global Ponzi scheme.'

Frank added. 'I could feel sorry for Bernie Madoff; he was sentenced to 150 years in jail when his Ponzi scheme knocked off a mere $65 Billion USD of investors funds; the rest of them walked away scot free with their Billions.'

'Why then are bank executives paid Billions?'

'Because they can get away with it. CEO's (Chief Executive Officers) put their friends on the Board and it's away to the races. Only now are shareholders beginning to wake up. The US Government tried to impose 90% tax on bonuses: unsuccessfully.'

'What ability do you need to be able to run a bank?'

'If you can count to ten you're in; with the widespread use of calculators you hardly need that ability unless you're playing golf.'

'What's happening now?' Ulick asked.

'The ECB as it's called has been credited with Trillions of euro; it will pay massive interest each year on the amount borrowed and in theory and in time will repay the capital. That will never happen; with their capital secure the money men only want their yearly interest.

At the present time the US national debt is a mere fifteen Trillion dollars and rising; it pays several hundred Billions in interest every year. The UK pays forty five Billion pounds a year in interest; Ireland East five Billion euro.'

'But don't the people know what's going on?' Ozzy asked.

'The people know only what they're told. The game is over for this time.'

'It will happen again?'

'Of course it will; the banks are bigger and more powerful now than ever.'

'How come the Big Money people have so much?' Ulick asked while Ozzy immersed himself in his pint.

'It's quite simple, Ulick. 10% of the people on this planet own 90% of our resources. They finance the world's Governments, the IMF, the World Bank, the ECB – you name it.

In the US 1% (that's 3 million people) own 90% of America's resources. (297 million people - 99% - own 10% of the country's resources)'

'What I want to know is why the little people are required to pay the bill?' Ozzy asked.

Frank replied. 'You surely don't think the Big Money people are going to pay; they're only interested in making more money out of our misery.'

'So, what's the solution?'

'The immediate solution; every country should default and go back to square one. The long term solution is a different form of exchange.'

'How could you have a different form of exchange?'

Frank replied. 'I hear tell there was a book published recently in which the author – maybe he's a half idiot – advocated replacing money with an internet points system where everyone would receive a fixed number of points each month.'

'You mean everyone on this planet?'

'Yes.'

'So everyone would be equal?'

'That's right.'

'That will never happen Frank.'

'It certainly won't in the short term; Big Money has too good a grip on the situation. But if we ever get to the stage where annual interest payable to bondholders or bailiffs as I call them, equals tax take, the whole system will collapse; big money will have committed financial suicide. In reality, the collapse will come long before that.'

***

What's our situation as a small country, Frank?'

'We're lucky; when we broke away from Dublin we started from scratch financially; we spend only what we've got.'

'We won't always have our oil revenues.'

'True but we're keeping those funds in reserve.'

'How do you do it then?

Frank smiled. 'We learned a lot from Dublin. As you know, ministers are selected by the Taoiseach of the day and don't have to be members of the Teac.'

'So they don't have to answer to Moxy and can't be bought?'

'Correct. They are people of ability there to do the job without fear or favour with no interest in the next election. They can only appoint one civil servant; Dublin has an army of civil servants that it can't get rid of.'

'I still can't see how you run the country with such a small number of people?'

'It's simple really; our integrated computer system makes it possible. We've increased the powers of the County Councils; they are now fully responsible for all activities within their areas including tax collection.'

'But County Councils are talking shops; some of the councillors would blather until the cows come home.'

Frank smiled.

'Why do you think they only meet one day a month with five months holidays; it's the permanent staff does the work and reports to the appropriate minister here in Galway.'

'How much are counsellors paid?'

'€50,000 a year.'

'And expenses?'

'It's all included in the €50,000. '

'And what about banking?'

'We set up the National Bank which is fully owned by the State. It's under the control of a specially appointed Minister who reports to the cabinet every month. It cannot borrow from other banks, do house mortgages or lend more that one per cent of its equity to any one client or company.

In the US banks are permitted by the SEC to borrow as much as they like; some have borrowed up to fifty times their capital which is a recipe for disaster. This practice is called leverage.'

'So our bank can only make a modest profit?'

'Money was invented as a means of exchange; it was never intended to become a commodity in its own right.'

'Who does the house mortgages then?'

'Specialist mortgages companies as in days of old; the borrowers pay the lenders, which keeps everyone on the straight and narrow. And no one in finance is permitted to earn more than a government minister.'

***

Voncrap was slightly less aggressive when he finally got to see the Taoiseach in Government buildings.

'Taoiseach, we have found our oil and will start moving our rig next month; we'll extend our pipe line and still use the refinery in Grange.'

Frank opened his file.

'Mr Voncrap, your concession is for blocks 106 to 109. The oil is in block 117. You have no concession for block 117.'

'It's still our oil.'

The Taoiseach remained cool; Voncrap was beginning to get hot under his highly starched collar.

'Mr Voncrap, it was never your oil. As drilling in blocks 106 to 109 has bottomed out you are now required under the terms of your contract to remove your oil rig and all other equipment from the site.'

'But it's our oil; in some way it moved further north.'

'The oil belongs to the people of this country. Your contract here is at an end. I'm now open to negotiation for the concession of block 117. It will be advertised shortly and you may bid if you're interested.'

He became angry. 'You can't do this; I'll sue your damned country for every euro you've got.'

The Taoiseach stood up. 'You do that; now get the hell out of my office.'

***

Shulter arrived early.

'Shaster in Bolivia has nationalised our oil company.'

'Can we organise a coupe there?'

He was doubtful. 'This fellow is very popular.'

'Arrange to have two Billion dollars lodged to his personal account from one of our Chinese banks and get me the documentation.'

'Yes sir.'

'And tell Yanbrety in Reykjavik, Iceland that I want the US Dollar only.'

***

The big blonde rough looking man who arrived at Galway International from New York looked like a tourist, but Rick Tabarst from New Jersey was no tourist. He passed through customs without any difficulty and took a taxi into town; after checking into the City Hotel he walked down to the docks and spent some time checking the liners. The one he was looking for hadn't arrived yet; it contained his skilfully packed high powered rifle. For a hit man with about twenty successes to his credit – he was losing count – he would have no difficulty fulfilling this contract.

In the morning, he hired a car and drove out into Connemara to have a look at Turla Lodge Hotel in Maam valley.

***

The master sent for Shulter.

'Instruct our hotel chain in China to borrow 100 Billion USD from Kin Lee's Hong Kong Bank, repayable in five years.'

'Yes sir.'

What's he up to now?

The master continued. 'What's happening in the Middle East?'

'Israel is keeping very quiet, too quiet for my liking. Lebanon, Syria, Iraq and Saudi are looking to buy arms. What should we do?'

The master thought about it for a moment.

'Supply them from our Indonesian plants – Saudi from Detroit.'

'Is there going to be a Middle East war sir?'

'I haven't decided yet.'

When Shulter departed the master sat down to consider the situation. A war in the Middle East might not be a bad thing provided he could persuade Russia and China to stay out of it. Then he would have to decide who should win that war; or would it be more advantageous from a financial point of view if it ended in stalemate?

***

John Polatley, the handsome young former senator from Ohio, sat down with his Secretary of State, Martha Kevioni in the Oval Office; he was cornered and he knew it.

'What am I going to do?'

'I wonder what Midas wants from a small country like Hi-Brasil sir.'

'I don't know but he's very determined and always gets his way.'

'So, we'll bomb Galway sir. We could say they're harbouring terrorists and have refused to hand them over.'

'I have a better idea; why don't we bomb the hotel where this bastard is staying and get rid of him for once and for all.'

'That's a great idea sir; if only we could afford it.'

***

Voncrap was in a more conciliatory frame of mind when the Taoiseach agreed to accept a visit from him. He had received legal advice that wasn't to his liking.

'Taoiseach, surely we can sort this out among ourselves. I've persuaded my board to increase your royalty to 10%. Isn't that a big improvement?'

'Do I look that green? I have two other oil companies offering 45%. You're wasting my time; I'll bid you good day.'

***

The master studied the urgent email received from his man in port Boston south which was formerly Byrd Station in western Antarctica; he rang Shulter.

'Get me President Polatley on the phone.'

The President came through almost immediately.

'John,' the master commenced. 'We have a problem in Antarctica. As you know one of my companies has been surveying land cleared by retreating ice.'

'I've been watching your progress with interest Herman; how much land is involved.'

'About 250,000 acres. The problem is an Australian warship has anchored off Boston south and ordered our people to leave as they are claiming this land for Australia.'

'What do you think we should do, Herman?'

'I want you to fly in a few thousand marines and take possession in the name of the United States; there are very valuable minerals in this area and as the ice retreats it's becoming more attractive.'

'I'll have to consult the Pentagon; how much time have we got?'

'You've got to move immediately; if the Australians land and take possession you could have a full scale war on your hands.'

'Leave it with me.'

***

Frank, sitting behind his desk in government buildings in Eyre Square, was alerted by the noise outside; he got up and walked to the window; he couldn't believe it; a massive fleet of heavy aircraft was approaching the city from the west. In the streets below everyone was going about their business unaware of the threat. It was too late to issue a warning; the aircraft crossed in over the city and then, to his astonishment, turned in a wide circle and flew back west. It was a warning.

He was furious; picked up the phone and asked his secretary to order the US ambassador attend on him immediately.

***

Herb Oxton, US Treasury Secretary, made a secret visit to Turla to see the master. The heavily built, affable former Professor of Economics at Harvard was in his second term in charge of the country's finances. Coffee served, the master wondered what merited such an unexpected visit; they met once before, at the President's inauguration.

'Sir,' he began, 'the President has asked me to seek your help; he's very concerned about those people who call themselves "Occupy Wall Street" because the movement is spreading rapidly not only in the US but throughout the world. We both feel we can't continue to ignore it.'

'What does he suggest?'

'Well sir the "Occupy" crowd have some merit in their case; the Wall Street people are out of control; they and the bankers are paying themselves far too much and compounding it by adding billions in bonuses.'

'But hasn't your President tried and failed to do anything about it.'

'True sir, but with your help he believes he can introduce some sanity into the situation.'

'What does he want to do this time?'

'He would like to send another Bill to Congress proposing a tax of 35% on all salaries over $1 million USD and a tax of 75% on all bonuses over $1 million USD. That would sort out Wall Street, put an end to this subversive movement and bring in a Trillion in badly needed extra tax.'

Herb Oxton knew the master had extensive banking interests although he couldn't identify them; a thorough international investigation had failed to come up with anything.

The master knew all about Oxton's efforts to identify his holdings; efforts that ran into the ground in his banks in Cayman, Zurich and Bermuda. He was quite pleased that his web of secrecy hadn't been penetrated.

The master took a pad off the desk and started scribbling.

'Let me suggest a better way of solving this problem.'

'Please do sir.'

'I think you should treat salary and bonus as income and tax it as follows: 35% on the first $2 million, 50% on the next $3 million and 99% on the balance. That would stop Billions being paid out in bonuses.'

'I agree sir, but we still need your assistance.'

'How can I help?'

'It's a numbers game sir; we've done the figures. We can get this through the Senate if we turn four senators.'

'You can identify them?'

'Yes sir.' He produced a list and handed it over.

The master studied it.

'They're Republican senators; the President cannot control his own party?'

'Unfortunately, that's true sir.'

'I'll need more information.'

Oxton produced a slim dossier from his briefcase and handed it over.'

The master perused it.

'I'll gladly assist if I can; leave it with me and I'll get back to you.'

His visitor smiled. 'Thank you sir. It's vital that we get this legislation through the house before the next election.'

***

Angelo Pistroni met Voncrap by arrangement in the bar of the Ardilaun Hotel; he ordered large brandies. Voncrap was in a bad mood and didn't think this meeting would do anything for him. He was wrong.

'What can you do for me holy man?' he demanded.

'Quite a lot,' he replied calmly. 'You want a new oil deal from Taoiseach Carney; I can get it for you.'

'That bastard is too damn greedy.'

He let that pass.

'He can afford it. He's got two other oil companies prepared to give him anything he wants. Let me be frank sir. He doesn't like you and unless I persuade him he won't give you a deal at any price.'

'I have to get this deal,' he paused and looked closely at him. 'What's in it for you?'

'I would like a contribution of a hundred million for my orders charities.'

'Get me the deal and I'll give you a hundred million.'

He ordered two more brandies.

***

Shulter listened carefully to the master's instructions.

'Withdraw our entire 100 Billion from Kin Lee's bank; get on to our rating agency and have them reduce his AAA rating to A.'

'Yes sir.'

'What are his shares currently quoted at?'

'700 Hong Kong Dollars.'

'When they fall to 300, use the 100 Billion withdrawn, and the 100 Billion borrowed by our Shanghai Group, to mount a dawn raid. When the purchase is completed instruct the rating agency to restore the AAA rating. That will teach the bastard not to meddle with his superiors.'

Shulter departed.

***

Frank got the tip off at midnight; he dressed quickly in his little apartment and headed for the office. Ulick joined him there. He was livid.

'A fleet of American long range bombers took off from New Jersey four hours ago heading north west.'

Ulick spoke quietly, 'Dan.'

He was there in a flash and listened while Frank outlined the problem.

'Can we warn the people?' he asked.

'There isn't time; they'll be here in less than half an hour. I've alerted the major rescue people and the hospitals.'

'Let's go out on the roof,' Ulick suggested and then turned to Frank. 'You had better drive out to Conna; you'll be safe there.'

'I'm not going anywhere.'

They made their way up the internal stairs and walked out on to the flat roof of the old railway hotel. Danny was angry but what could he do to save his people? It was a bright moonlit night. They watched in silence. Then they heard the faint drone as the fleet of bombers approached over Galway Bay.

'They're flying too high to be identified,' Ulick remarked.

'At about 20,000 feet,' Frank guessed.

Then, still off shore they released their bombs. Danny held up his hands and screamed,' Bombs, do not touch this land.'

They watched while thousands of bombs headed towards the city; suddenly they changed course and fell into Galway Bay in a series of explosions, sending mighty gushers of water high in the sky. They assembled into a tornado which caused such atmospheric imbalance that the shock wave blew several aircraft off course; three of them were forced to make emergency landings at Galway International where they were immediately impounded.

Ulick hugged the little man.

'You saved us lad, you saved us lad.'

Frank lifted Danny up in his arms and all three of them danced around the roof.

***

The American ambassador was angry too; he received no warning of the raid and if it had been successful he could have been one of the casualties. Learning that three American crews and their aircraft were impounded at Galway International he had to think fast. Shown into the Taoiseach's presence he was received by a very frosty Frank Carney who gave him a tongue lashing that broke all the rules of polite diplomacy. Eventually he got the opportunity to speak.

'Taoiseach, my government apologises profusely for this near disaster. You will receive a full apology and compensation from President Polatley. That fleet of aircraft was on a training flight testing out new navigational equipment; it was supposed to be over the North Pole where obsolete bombs were to be disposed of.'

'Do you expect me to believe that bullshit?'

'Taoiseach, do you think I would have stayed in the city last night if I knew this raid was planned?'

'I have a mind to arrest that fellow in Turla and throw him in jail.'

The Ambassador became agitated.

'Please don't do that.'

'You make damn sure there are no more raids on my country.'

'I will sir, but it would be better if you give the master what he wants.'

He paused. 'Will you accept our apology and release our personnel?'

'I'll think about it,' Frank growled.

***

The master put aside the dossier and considered his options; would supporting the President's bill be advantageous to him financially or otherwise, He had known for years that the people who ran his banks were insufferable arrogant over sexed alpha snobs; he could only deal with them by showing his hand; that he wouldn't do.

This Bill would eliminate the massive bonuses being paid to those people and add Billions to his banks' profits. There would be no downside; he didn't draw any salary or bonus and only paid his staff once a year from one of his offshore banks. In fact he didn't handle money; all bills were sent to one of his companies. He would continue to operate tax free.

He had enormous armament factories in the states represented by the four senators; President Polatley would know that. He sent an email to his man in Washington who kept tabs on the Congress for him. His instructions were clear; tell these four gentlemen that failure to support the Bill would mean the loss of their factories and their seats in the Senate. And tell the president that he wouldn't approve any further restrictions on derivates; there had to be a quid pro quo.

***

Senior Brother Angelo sat by the lake with Lurglurg; it was a lovely sunny morning in Connemara with a light breeze blowing across the lake.

'Lurglurg,' Angelo began, 'I'm delighted to see you're enjoying good health. You're doing a great job here and I hope you'll continue for many years to come.'

He tried a smile.

'I love this place; it has a serenity that reminds me of my early days on Aran. And apart from a visit to the clinic in Moycullen last year I'm in good shape.'

'Why did you visit the clinic?'

'To have my appendix removed; they still send for me once a month for a check up.'

Angelo thought this was a bit odd but didn't say so.

'I'm sure you find those visits a bit of a burden.'

He was going to say a bit of a pain but didn't think it appropriate.

'I really enjoy my monthly visit. Sister Agatha, a lovely nun meets me and takes me to Dr Jennings. He hardly looks at me. Then I'm taken to Sister Agatha's drawing room and we have tea and sandwiches.'

Angelo felt he was getting the picture; he was fairly sure that Lurglurg wasn't.

'What age is Sister Agatha?'

'I don't know, about my age I suppose.'

'Why don't you invite her to visit here for a week as your guest?'

'Do you think she would come?'

'I'm sure she would be delighted.'

***

The master reluctantly granted Angelo Pistroni another audience. Re-alising it might be a very short one he didn't waste the great man's time. Danny wandered around the room; what's going on now?

'Sir, I believe I can help you.' Angelo began.

The master looked at him disdainfully.

'I know the purpose of your visit to this country.'

He didn't believe him.

'And what is that purpose?'

He extracted a sheet of paper from his pocket and handed it over. The master looked at it and handed it back; it seemed that a meeting of the minds might now take place.

'Why would you do this for me?' he inquired.

'Sir, as you know, I represent the charitable wing of our order. We are having a really difficult time in Africa; a further subscription would help.'

'If you can deliver I'll give you ten million dollars.'

Angelo looked distinctly unhappy.

'I was hoping for a Billion sir.'

'That's a lot of money.'

'But look what you're getting for it.'

'Oh all right.'

'I assume sir there will be no more attacks on Galway?'

The master considered it.

'I'll cancel the planned missile strike. But don't delay, I've already spent too much time in this desolate country.'

'In these situations a payment up front would be usual.'

'I'll have Shulter attend to it; it's a charitable donation, that's all he needs to know.'

It occurred to the master that Shulter might think he was getting religion; not that he saw anything wrong with religion. In fact it was a very good thing; it kept the hoi poloi (the great unwashed) under control.

***

The master took a phone call from Martha Kevioni. No way would Israel agree to his suggestion that they give up their nuclear bombs if Iran did.

'Don't let Israel bomb Iran,' he instructed and hung up.

Now he would implement his master plan for the Middle East; control of NuclearE was crucial to it. He emailed his instructions to his man in Istanbul and made a point of not being available when Martha Kevioni rang later.

The announcement, when it came, made world headlines: TURKEY, SYRIA, SAUDI ARABIA AND EGYPT GOING NUCLEAR. Israel was furious and very direct; they would go to war if necessary to prevent these countries having nuclear. American Secretary of State, Martha Kevioni was adamant; the United States would not permit this, but didn't threaten war.

The master was delighted; in one hour he had stabilised the Middle East for at least ten years. All the talk and bluster about Iran would now stop; sanctions end and the region return to a noisy peace. It would take quite some time to achieve and would add Billions to NuclearE's profits.

Including Syria was particularly provocative; in its current state of flux that country wouldn't be able to afford nuclear for at least another twenty years. He would now insist on a separate Palestinian state.

He was very sympathetic, but not helpful, when Martha Kevioni eventually got to speak to him.

'Madame Secretary, once Israel refused to even talk to Iran this was bound to happen.'

'It dramatically increases instability in the region.'

'I don't agree Madame; let them all have the bomb. They daren't use it anyway. Iran couldn't use the bomb against Israel without destroying their Palestinian friends.'

'We've got to stop them. I've already spoken to the French President. He will not permit their nuclear plant companies to become involved.'

The master took that undertaking with Lot's salt.

Madame continued. 'I've also spoken to Herr Lutzgart in Berlin. He tells me control of NuclearE is no longer in German hands. Can you find out who owns it now?'

'I'll certainly try Madame.'

'I'll keep in touch. This is a very bad day for America.' She paused. 'The President wants to speak to you.'

***

John Polatley was triumphant.

'Herman, ten thousand of our marines were airlifted into Boston South earlier today. They were just in time; the entire Australian fleet was moving into the area with a view to putting troops ashore. This is our territory; the US flag flies over the city; the seventh fleet is on its way south.'

'That's a good result,' the master responded calmly. 'Have there been any diplomatic repercussions?'

'Australian PM Harris is furious and insists it's their territory. He's demanding an international conference to decide the future of Antarctica.'

'Good. You should claim the entire continent for the US.'

'I'll do that.'

'Let me know before you proceed with the missile attack on Galway; it may not be necessary.'

'I'll keep in touch.' He rang off.

Shulter arrived.

'Australia is looking to buy missiles from a number of our factories.'

'Offer terms but don't do anything.'

'I don't understand sir.'

'If we refuse they will approach China; by the time they find out we're not going to supply, the emergency will be over.'

'Yes sir.'

***

In the long term future the new continent of Anctartica, twice the area of Australia, would be a major project. He had already invested heavily in New Boston city with port facilities for the enormous imports necessary to cater for a population of 10,000 people in such an inhospitable climate. As the ice retreated he increased his scientific teams; the international airport facilitated travel and, except during winter storms, operated normally.

The new continent, unseen by humans for millions of years, with its mountain range dividing it in two, would be unveiled over the next twenty years; a treasure trove of minerals. The down side: the world's oceans would rise by three metres and about 10% of land elsewhere would be lost. He had already set up a committee to identify assets which should be moved to higher ground.

One of his scientific teams was looking at the feasibility of building an underground railway system right across the continent linking underground cities. President Polatley thought this new 53rd State was American; it wasn't, it was his and America would be required to provide whatever backup he needed.

The international squabbling would go on for years; China, Russia, India, Australia and Argentina (at least) would want a piece of this valuable property. He would finance all of them; should the US not succeed in getting the entire continent he would control the other occupiers.

***

Rick Tabarst, complete with pack lunch and fishing rod, set up camp every day in the bushes across the lake from Turla Lodge. He spent his time studying the front of the hotel through his binoculars; eventually he caught sight of the master on the third floor. This would be an easy hit when the target stepped out on to the balcony. He kept his high powered rifle in the boot of the car nearby.

In the course of his wanderings Danny spotted the fisherman; he looked harmless enough.

***

Shulter arrived holding a sheaf of papers.

'A few queries sir.'

The master put down his coffee.

'Fire ahead.'

'The Mexican drugs baron has approached our New York secondary bank; he wants to launder $80 Billion USD. He plans to make the freshly laundered money available to a well known bondholder.'

'Pass it to our Panama bank and give him 20%.'

'He's looking for 50%.'

'Tell him to go to hell; he's getting greedy. Last time he got 18%.'

Shulter made a note.

'Argentina is looking for a massive arms purchase; I think they're going to have another go at the Falklands.'

'I have oil interests in the Falklands.'

'So we should refuse to supply?'

'Pass the order to our Brazilian factory and long date it – cash up front. Let London know; tell them to make sure they hold the Falklands.'

Shulter referred to his notes.

'Japan has approached NuclearE; they want a manufacturing plant to be set up in Osaka.'

'That's a good idea; will they finance it?'

'Yes.'

'Go ahead then.'

***

Frank Carney met Angelo Pistroni for a quiet drink in Paulo's; it was mid afternoon with only a few customers slaking their thirst. Sitting on the counter beside them the unseen Danny listened carefully. After a few moments they were joined by Ulick; Paulo put up three brandies and left them to it.

'Ulick,' Frank began, 'Angelo thinks Kingpa should give Midas what he's asked for.'

Ulick turned to the Senior Brother. 'Are you serious? Give that lunatic immortality?'

Frank put down his glass. 'We're damned if we do and damned if we don't.' He paused. 'I can't put our people in Galway at risk again; if Danny hadn't saved us the city would now be a pile of rubble.'

Angelo tried to reassure him.

'Midas may rule the world now but things change. The present system can't last; the lunatic might lose all his power.'

'I would like to think this Occupy Wall Street movement is only the beginning,' Frank added.

Ulick disagreed. 'They have no chance. We have to remove this threat from our people.'

The little man decided it was time to join them; he needed a pint anyway. In the door walked Ozzy to be brought quickly up to date while he demolished his pint.

'What do you think?' Frank asked him.

'I'll ask Kingpa.'

***

Shulter reported in.

'There's uproar in La Paz, Bolivia; Shaster denies that he received a bribe of 2 Billion USD; says he's been set up by America.'

'Will he give me back my oil fields?'

'He absolutely refuses.'

'Has the CIA talked with the leader of the opposition?'

'He's amenable, but it will cost a Billion in a Swiss bank.'

The master was disgusted. 'It's becoming harder to find an honest man in this crazy world. Go ahead.'

'Langley reckons there will be a civil war.'

'He shouldn't have taken my oil.'

***

Danny visited the master's suite and watched the great man in action. This morning, with the world media speculation firmly concentrated on the Middle East, he decided that a war between Russia and China would be bad for business at this time. Iran was off the radar; oil prices would remain stable for the present. China and Russia would support the four new nuclear states; there would no question of military action by either Israel or America.

By now American satellites would have picked up the Chinese army in Mongolia and Russian forces facing them across the border. Odd that he hadn't been told. America regarded China, now the biggest economy in the world, as their greatest threat. It had built up a massive army, although as he knew, not fully up to date. Its fourth aircraft carrier was launched in Shanghai two weeks earlier. But the big question remained; was the built up for offence or defence?

The American high command, the strutting generals, wanted to take on China; had they already forgotten Vietnam, Iraq and Afghanistan? Such a conflict would be a disaster for the world. He had instructed the US President to cultivate good relations with Russia, Japan, the Philippines and India; the Chinese would know better than to take on such a combination.

If Taiwan declared independence China would invade; it was inevitable. He had instructed President Polatley that America could make noise when this happened: not war.

With the big decisions out of the way he had a coffee and wondered which of his ladies he should invite next. In a relaxed and peaceful frame of mind he stepped out on to his balcony and surveyed the surrounding lakes and mountains. At that instant he should have died.

Danny heard the high velocity bullet heading for the master. Instinctively, he waved his little hand and the bullet passed harmlessly over the roof. Knowing where it came from, he was there before a second one could be fired. Tabarst couldn't believe his first shot failed; he lined up his sights again.

Danny kicked him in the shin, grabbed the rifle, stood back and pointed it at the hit man. Tabarst's eyes opened wide in terror; the gun was doing this all by itself; he waited for the end. The gun now pointed to his car and followed him; he jumped in behind the wheel and, sweating profusely, fiddled around for his keys. He put down the boot while Danny fired two shots in the air and found himself sitting on the ground. Getting up, he threw the gun into the lake.

Then he stopped to think; should he have saved the master?

***

The Taoiseach signed all three copies of the new oil concession and passed the documents over to Voncrap who signed them and put one copy in his brief case. Danny was there keeping a watchful eye on proceedings.

Afterwards they shook hands and the Taoiseach warned Voncrap.

'Do not outline the details until I've addressed the Teac.'

Voncrap was so relieved that he actually smiled.

'Whatever you say, Taoiseach.'

They shook hands and he departed.

***

The master received the Taoiseach with due respect this time and shook Ozzy's hand warmly. Having been told his wish was granted he would only accept confirmation from the man who walked the water. He led the way into his sitting room where three brandies awaited them. He turned politely to them and raised his glass; 'Good health; do I get a certificate?'

Ozzy smiled. 'Kingpa, the King of our ancient people, says no; you must not tell anyone; if others learn of this honour they may seek it too.'

'Good thinking.'

Ozzy smiled again. 'Kingpa say you must pay this country one Billion euro every year.'

Shulter mustn't know about this and he didn't like instalment payments except when receiving them. He took out his cheque book.

'I'll do better than that; I'll write a cheque now for fifty Billion. I'll do it again every fifty years.'

In fifty years time these fellows would be long gone; the question of further payments wouldn't arise.

He wrote the cheque and handed it to the Taoiseach.

They shook hands and parted.

The master sent for Shulter.

'Get my plane into Shannon; we will fly to my island home tomorrow.'

He paused. 'And check that land deal in Sweden.'

'Yes sir. The two Sudan states are looking to buy arms; looks like a civil war.'

'Put them in touch with our factory in the Philippines – cash up front.'

***

When Angelo rang Voncrap for payment of his 100 million USD he received a curt reply.

'I have no agreement with you unless it's in writing; go to hell holy man.' He slammed down the phone smiling.

An hour later he received a phone call from the Taoiseach.

'Voncrap, as you did not honour your agreement with Pistroni, I'm shredding the document you signed in my office yesterday. This concession will now go to the Oxyl Corporation.'

'You can go to hell, I have the contract which was signed in your office; it's water tight.'

'That's odd, I have the three copies of the now defunct agreement on my desk, so I'll bid you good day.'

He put down the phone. It should be said that at Angelo's suggestion Danny had skilfully relieved Voncrap of his copy.

Five minutes later Voncrap rang back, a very different Voncrap this time.

'My apologies, Taoiseach. I had completely forgotten about my promise to Pistroni. I'll send him a cheque for 100 million USD immediately. I seem to have mislaid my copy; will you give a copy to my courier?'

'You'll have to send 200 million to Angelo; he's very annoyed that you tricked an innocent churchman.'

'There was no agreement for 200.'

'Well then you can send him 300 million.'

'This is blackmail.'

'Call it what you will. You can now send him 400 million.'

'Stop please. I'll send him 400 million USD.'

'You'll send him 400 million Sterling by way of a non negotiable draft to be in his possession before four o'clock this afternoon. If I haven't his confirmation before I rise to address the Teac you can kiss Block 117 and your ass goodbye.'

Frank hung up smiling and turned to Ulick. 'At the Louisburg fair I learned it there.'

***

Voncrap's announcement of the new oil concession on block 117 was long on euphoria but short on detail. Even so, his company's shares rose dramatically on Wall Street. On the grapevine Moxy heard there was little change in the royalty to be paid to the state. He looked forward to the meeting of the Teac; Carney would have no option now but to call a General Election.

The Taoiseach, after a phone call from Angelo, took his seat in the packed assembly. The media had already poured cold water on the deal because the Taoiseach refused to make any comment. Ulick was sitting quietly in the visitors' gallery. The Teac was called to order; Frank rose.

'Comairle, as the oil exploration concession on blocks 106 to 109 in the Celtic sea has expired, we have concluded a new agreement with the Voncrap Corporation for drilling to commence in three months time in block 117 which is off the Donegal coast. The new agreement is more beneficial to our country; block 117 is believed to contain 100 Billion barrels of good quality oil.'

Moxy interrupted him.

'What royalty Taoiseach?'

He ignored him and continued.

'Our Minister for Energy has expressed satisfaction at the terms achieved; a copy of the contract will be available for inspection in our publications office tomorrow.'

Moxy jumped up.

'Stop waffling Taoiseach and tell the Teac how much royalty we're getting?'

Frank picked up a copy of the contract and pretended to root through it.

'Oh yes, here it is. Deputy O'Shea we're getting 35% royalty per barrel on the first 10 Billion barrels, increasing to 40% from there on.'

His deputies rose and gave him a standing ovation that went on until the Comairle called the Teac to order. Moxy nearly died but he wasn't finished yet.

'You failed to get a deposit up front Taoiseach.'

He referred to the contract wording again.

'I'm sure it's here somewhere. Yes, here it is.'

He stood up straight and held up the document.

'We have received a deposit of ten Billion euro.'

He sat down while he received another standing ovation.

When the Teac settled down the Comairle called on Moxy O'Shea who addressed the house with stinging indignation.

'You call that a victory, a mere 35%? It's our oil 100%. I wouldn't have settled for less than 60%. I think it's clear to everyone here that you don't know what you're doing; dissolve the Teac Taoiseach and let the people elect a government that will serve them honestly and fairly. What happened to that great project, the new Clifden railway? Why are the plans gathering dust in the Minister's office? What happened to your pious hopes of reducing taxes? What happened to your promise to add an extra wing to the Moycullen clinic?'

He sat down amid cheers from his members.

Frank rose.

'Comairle, the government has allocated ten Billion euro to the Clifden and Roundstone railway system. The work will commence as soon as contractors are appointed and the necessary contracts signed.'

'More wild promises,' Moxy roared.

The Taoiseach ignored him.

'In the construction stage there will be a massive increase in employment; the new railway company will employ 1,000 permanent staff.'

He paused and looked around him.

'This new state of the art modern facility will be a major boost to our tourist industry. I would like to see a railway running from Westport via Louisburg via Leenane to join up with the Clifden line at Maam Cross and then via Costello and Spiddal into Galway.'

He paused again.

'I think you're right Deputy O'Shea; we've been in government for nearly three years now. We've served the people to the best of our ability. I'm now dissolving the Teac and calling a General Election which will be held three weeks from today.'

His members gave him yet another standing ovation. Moxy looked sick.

***

The Taoiseach's arrival in Paulo's was greeted with loud cheers; Ulick, Angelo and Ozzy were there already. Paulo was jubilant as he served large brandies on the house.

'Taoiseach you've put us on the map; I'll be able to travel into Galway by train. How soon?'

'It will take about three years.'

Ulick was still concerned about the master.

'Have we inflicted a monster on the world?' he asked Ozzy.

The old man smiled. 'I don't think so.'

'But Kingpa has given him what he asked for.'

'That's true but he didn't give him what he wanted.'

Angelo came to Ozzy's rescue. 'Let me elucidate: the master demanded immortality by which he meant the gift of being able to live here forever; we all have immortality but we don't have it here.'

'So Kingpa didn't give him anything he didn't already have.'

'Correct.'

'What happens when he finds out?'

'It will be too late then won't it?'

Paulo served another round of brandies and filled one for himself.

'What are we going to do with all this money?' Ulick asked.

Frank turned to Angelo. 'Did you sell the shares?'

'I did; we made Billions.'

'What's going on?' Ulick demanded.

Angelo smiled. 'It's a long story. When Voncrap lost out in blocks 106 to 109 I realised his company's shares would go through the floor.'

'Who told you that was happening?'

He put his hand on Ozzy's shoulder. 'My good friend Dan Ozzy here.'

'Go on.'

'I contacted my broker in New York and told him to buy when the shares hit rock bottom.'

He smiled at Frank. 'It was a close run thing; I had to keep Voncrap on board. You played a blinder getting me an extra 300 million, sterling at that.'

The Taoiseach looked astutely at Angelo.

'And to think Voncrap thought you were a fool. What are you going to do with all that money?'

'I'm donating 200 million to the clinic in Moycullen for a new wing and the balance goes to Africa Aid.'

'You're some operator.'

'I couldn't have done it without Ozzy here. I've really enjoyed my visit; now I'm heading back to my dear wife and family in Jamaica.'

Ozzy smiled benignly. 'You will always be welcome here.'

Ulick scratched his head. 'Frank, what about the 100 Billion you got from the master? How do you explain that?'

'Simple. It's a donation from an anonymous donor.'

'What will you use it for?'

Frank grinned. 'I'll use it to fulfil the dream of a lifetime; to build the Westport Galway Railway line. I'll be able to travel to the Teac in style.'

'And break your journey in Conna,' Ulick added.

Reluctantly Angelo decided it was time to go; he shook their hands and smiled.

'There must be other suckers out there who would pay good money for immortality.'

In great glee they escorted him to the door where Sister Agatha, Lurglurg and the brothers were waiting to say goodbye to this most unusual churchman; After many hugs, cheers and some tears he got into his waiting taxi.

THE END